Ooh-la-la
(MAX IN LOVE)

Allo? Allo Jacques?
Jacques, it is me, Mimi.
Oui. Oui. Mimi. I just got off
the phone with Kiki.
Oh Jacques, not Fifi, Kiki.
Listen. Zouzou called Loulou,
Loulou called Coco,
Coco called Kiki,
and Kiki called me me.
Have you heard the latest?
Tout Paris is abuzz. Max is here!
Who is Max??? Mon dieu!
Sacre bleu! He is the coolest cat,
I mean the hottest dog.
He is Max Stravinsky.
The dog poet from New York.
That bohemian beagle. He's
staying at Madame Camembert's.
I don't know what he's going
to do, but I will call Tarte.
Tarte Tatin. She finds out
everything from that bogus
Barcelonian baron,
Federico de Potatoes,
who is a fortune hunter or
a fortune teller or something,
but he is très intelligent and
he always gives her the scoop.
Alors, I must run.
My soufflé is sinking.
Jacques, there is something
in the air. Don't you think?
I feel it is very, oh so very . . .

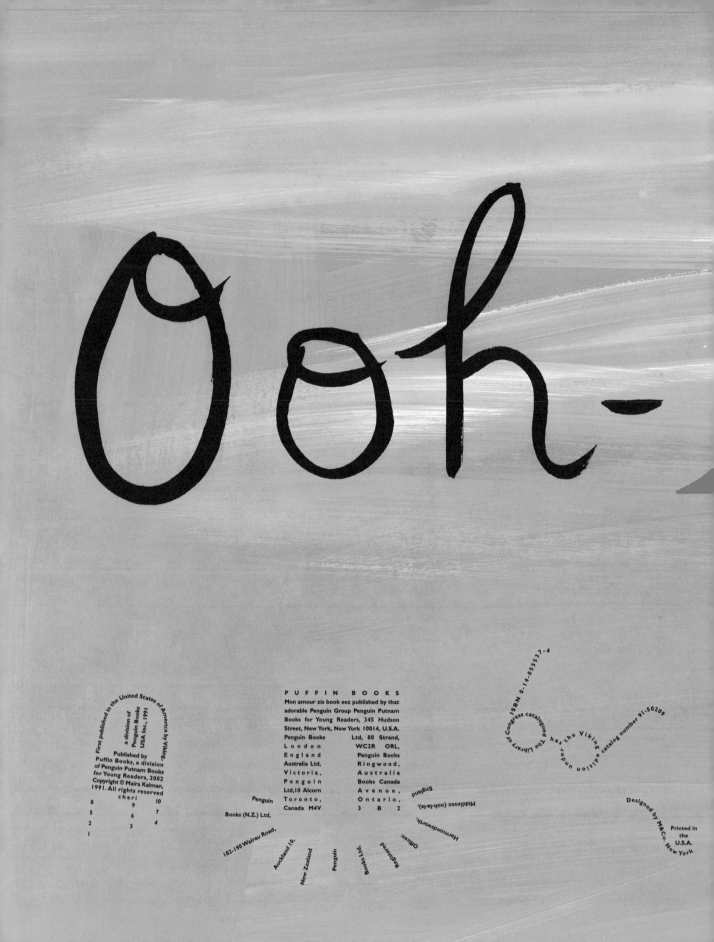

Ooh-

First published in the United States of America by Viking,
a division of
Penguin Books
USA Inc., 1991

Published by
Puffin Books, a division
of Penguin Putnam Books
for Young Readers, 2002
Copyright © Maira Kalman,
1991. All rights reserved

cheri

8   9   10
5   6   7
2   3   4
1

PUFFIN BOOKS
Mon amour zis book eez published by that
adorable Penguin Group Penguin Putnam
Books for Young Readers, 345 Hudson
Street, New York, New York 10014, U.S.A.
Penguin Books   Ltd, 80 Strand,
London   WC2R ORL,
England   Penguin Books
Australia Ltd,   Ringwood,
Victoria,   Australia
Penguin   Books Canada
Ltd,10 Alcorn   Avenue,
Toronto,   Ontario,
Canada M4V   3 B 2

Penguin
Books (N.Z.) Ltd,

182-190 Wairau Road,

Auckland 10,

New Zealand

Penguin

Books Ltd,

Registered

Offices:

Harmondsworth,

Middlesex (ooh-la-la),

England

ISBN 0-14-055537-4

The Library of Congress catalogued the Viking edition under the catalog number 91-50209

Designed by M&Co. New York

Printed in
the
U.S.A.

ooh-la-la

(MAX IN LOVE)

MAIRA KALMAN

For Venus
Pluto,
and
T
i
b
o
r
Kalman

Mer
ci
beau
coup
to M.
Jacques
Tati and
mille fleurs
to Scott
Marquis de
Stowell

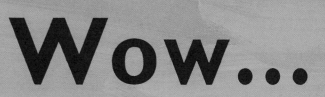

Wow...

My room was the Blue Suite
or as the French say,
"Bleu."

Bleu walls.

Bleu bed.

Bleu chair.

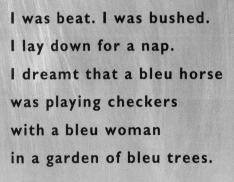

I was beat. I was bushed.
I lay down for a nap.
I dreamt that a bleu horse
was playing checkers
with a bleu woman
in a garden of bleu trees.

The sky was pink.

Go figure.

I was awakened by a k-k-**k**-**k**-knocking at the door.
In entered a

longmustache

followed by a man.

"Bonjour, Monsieur Max,
allow me to introduce myself.
I am Fritz from the Ritz
which I quit in a snit
when the chef in a fit
threw escargot on my chapeau
and hit my head
with a stale French bread.
Now I am here
in this little hôtel
run by the aromatic
Madame Camembert.
I adore her and
she adores me.
It's not always
that simple
in this town
of Paree."

With that, he placed
a tray on my bed.
"I thought you might
need this." He was right.
I was so hungry
I could have
eaten my beret.

As I was eating, my **eyes** fell on an amazing building outside my window.

Fritz," I asked, "what's that scary looking shack with those creepy monsters sticking out?"

"That *shack* monsieur, is the great **Notre-Dame Cathedral** and those 'monsters' are gargoyles. A hunchback used to live in that tower. And he died of a broken heart. And now I will leave you to your ruminations. Au revoir."

I gazed out the window and wondered.
About love.

The door, she knocked.
Entered a woman, walking a leopard.

"non"

"My name is
Charlotte Russe.
I came by autobus.
I am your French tutor.
But you are a chien! A dog!
Well never mind.
I have taught plenty of rats
in my time so I can
certainly teach a dog.
 Now. Put this clothes pin
on your nose,
 make your mouth, ze bouche,
into a little bonbon shape.
 Put your hands on your hips,
stamp your foot and say, 'Non.
Non.Non.Non.Non.Non.'
Now say 'ooh la la.' That's it.
'Ooh la la and non.'"
Suddenly she flung
herself on the bed
crying, "Monsieur Max,
I cannot teach today.
I just fell in love and
I cannot concentrate."

With that she left.
What a lovesick town.

I was
itchy
to walk

through
the boulevards,
the parks, and
the little streets
on that
sunlit day.

To inhale leafy lilacy Paris.

It was April after all.

I decided I must see Mona Lisa, who is not a friend,
but a painting by Leonardo da Vinci.
Everyone in the world comes to Paris, runs to the museum,
stands on line for five or six hundred hours and then they all go
ooooh ooooh ooooh and ahhhhhh.

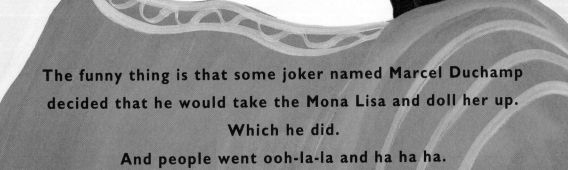

The funny thing is that some joker named Marcel Duchamp
decided that he would take the Mona Lisa and doll her up.
Which he did.
And people went ooh-la-la and ha ha ha.

As I left the museum,
I saw a scene that made my heart stand still.
A man had written poems all over
the sidewalk and the buildings and the cars
and the trees. As the cars left, parts of
his poems went whizzing around Paris,

and as the leaves fell from the trees,
words fluttered down to the ground.

I kept walking.
I was in a funny mood.
Expecting something I couldn't name.

"Allo Jacques. It's moi, Mimi.
What a horrible day.
The butcher delivered
the wrong order.
Instead of sixty spicy saucissons
and a small steak
for my dog Sutzi
they delivered sixty steaks
and one sweet saucisson.
Then Louis L'Amour came over
and cried for three hours
about his beloved Lula Fabula
who ran away with the circus
to become a snake charmer.
Quelle kook.
But the latest on Max. He has
been seen everywhere with a
hangdog expression on his face
and if I know anything,
which I do,
this moody meandering means
one thing.
Love, Jacques. L'amour.
He is looking for,
needy of, and pining for love.
Lovelovelovelove is in the air.
Isn't it glorious, Jacques?
But I must dash.
My mousse is melting.
Byebye."

I had walked like crazy
when I suddenly came upon it.
It. The tinker toy tower.
The Eiffel Tower.
As I took the elevator up

up,
up

I looked
down

down

down
at the vista below, thinking of
the kings and queens, poets and
artists who had lived and loved
in this city. And I wondered
who invented the soufflé
anyway? And what
was he thinking?

A t-t-tap on my shoulder broke my reverie.

"Excusez-moi, but aren't you Max Stravinsky?"

"Yes," I answered brilliantly.

"I am Pierre Potpourri, the owner of the
Crazy Wolf Nightclub.
Monsieur Max, would you grace us
with your presence tonight
at the Crazy?"

"Yes," I answered dramatically.

"Capital. Now you must
join me for lunch.
I am meeting a
dear friend,
Madame
Melba."

The Peach.   La Pêche.   Everyone knew Peach Melba.
She owned the world famou
Glamour Puss Charm School.
She had two French bulldogs
on her lap who were having
a terrible argument
about philosophy.

"Idiote, imbécile, stupide!!"
they barked at each other.
Next to Melba was her
constant companion,
a monkey named Sammy
who was wearing
an enormous feather
in his hat which he used
to tickle people's ears.

"**Charrrrrmed** to meet you,
Mr. Shostakovitch," trilled
Melba as I bowed hello.
"Stravinsky," I said.
"The name is Stravinsky."
"Oh of course,
Mr. Stradivarius,
of course. Absurd mistake."

We all ordered soup du jour
and ate in peace until one
of the dogs dumped his soup
on the other one's head.
Lunch lunched, Melba toaste
we decided to go to the . .

They had the most
amazing hairdos from
all these guys who
flipped their wigs.

Pompadour Museum.

I headed back to the hotel.
On my way I saw
a pair of black shoes
sitting on the sidewalk.
Next to them stood
a fish-eyed man in his socks
looking up at the sky.

Back in my room,
the phone, he rang.
"Allo, zis eez
Monsieur Max,"
I said Frenchily.

"Hey, Max, what's with the phoney baloney French accent? It's me, Leon. Your devoted agent. While you stuff your face with french fries, I'm working like a dog making deals for you. And baby, this is it. The sweetest deal of all. I'm in Hollywood and they want you to write a script. Some cockamamie love story. They want you here pronto to start writing. You'll love it here. Everyone is beautiful. Love ya, Maxie. Ciao."

I hung up.
Leon sounded so
strange. The Cinema had
appeal. But something
was missing. How could
I write a love story if
I didn't have . . . love?

"Allo, alloooooo Jacques,
can you hear me? What is all
that wailing in the background?
Did you hear the latest? Max
had lunch with Peach Melba.
She runs that glamour school.
You must have seen her ads:
'Do Not Be a Sour Puss
Do Not Suck on Lemons
You Can Be a Glamour Puss
In a Makeover Made in Heaven.'
She charges an arm and a leg
and teaches people how to
dress walk talk eat breathe
and in the end, VOILÀ!
From a pig to a princess!!
Tonight?
I am going to the Crazy Wolf,
of course. Tout Paris
will be there. Max is coming.
Crêpes Suzette is performing.
Yes. That divine dalmation.
What will I wear?
You know that monkey, Sammy?
Yes, Sammy Lacroix. He is the
most brilliant fashion designer
and he has created this
fabulous frock made out of
bananas. Yes, only bananas.
But Jacques, I must run.
My bunches are beginning
to droop."

The night came. With stars. Down a crooked flight of stairs and a crooked alley a crooked I knocked three times on a small green door and I was in the Crazy Wolf. That noise-soaked, blue-smoked spot.

Hey, fermez la porte, someone shouted. Hey, fermez la bouche, someone else shouted.

Quelle scene.

Suddenly a large wolf wearing a suit
came running toward me.
I nearly jumped to the chandelier.
'Max, it's me, Pierre,"
said the wolf, taking off his headdress.
"Welcome Max. We are about to begin the show.
Ladies and gentlemen, the
incomparable **Crêpes Suzette.**"

All eyes turned
toward the stage.
The star-splattered,
peacock blue curtains
parted slowly.
A blue spotlight
curled down to
a black piano,
and there,
bathed in
that light,
was the dog
I had been
looking for
my whole life.

My insides were on fire.
I was smitten.
I was bitten.
I was in love.
She closed her eyes.
Her elegant paws with
her neatly manicured claws
began to play.
A Chopin ballade,
a smattering
of Smetana,
a medley
of Mozart.

As she finished,
the transported audience
burst into a frenzy of applause.
"Merci beaucoup,"
she murmured demurely.

I was clickering.
I wanted to run and hide.
The poem I had prepared
seemed meaningless.
CHAIRS? Who cared
about chairs? I tore up
the old poem and
jumped onto the stage.

Oh
my hootchie
kootchie
poochie
your hotty
spotty
body
makes me tingle with joy.
You played the legato,
my heart went staccato.
My musical muse
no longer confused,
I have found
my raison d'être.
It is you,
my Crêpes Suzette.

The rest, as they say,
is history. Crêpes is
coming with me to Hollywood.
She will compose
the music for my movie.
Our last day in Paris
we led the **Dog Day Parade**.
I read the poem I had
written for this occasion:

In chic Paree
the chicest day
is when the dogs stroll down
the Champs Elysées.
Great danes romancing,
pink poodles prancing.
It's swank
it's grand
it's pooch couture.
They saunter with style
about half a mile
and end up at Maxims,
that most marvelous spot
for champagne and caviar
and a little whatnot.
A toast to life
A toast to love
Salut! Olé!
We're off to L.A.!

"Allo.
Oh JacquesJacquesJacquesJacques
What a night it was.
Quelle nuit.
It was the night of love.
Before our eyes Max and
Crêpes became a dog duet.
Paw in paw they strolled
through Paris. But now,
they are sailing for Hollywood
on the Toujours L'Amour.
Oh Jacques, I feel so sad.
So empty. So triste.
Jacques, why do you never
say anything?
All I do is talktalktalktalktalk
to you and you hardly ever
utter a word and I . . .
What? WHAT??
Oh Jacques, I am stunned.
I am completely speechless
and I am trying to
think of something to say
but I cannot because
my mind is swirling and twirling
and . . .
What?
Yes Jacques. Yes. So simple.
Yes, of course I can say that.
Yes, Jacques. I love you."

Ze end.

Maira

Kalman was born at a young age in
Tel Aviv near the ocean under the stars. At
the age of four she moved with her family (of
course) to the hard gray
city of New York
with hamburg-
ers and onions
frying on the
griddle. She
began to
dance, then to
play the
piano, then to
write, then to
paint.

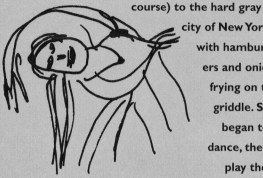

She stopped
dancing and playing
the piano, but kept the
writing and painting stuff.

She has
written
and illus-
trated ten
children's
books
including
*Max
Makes
a Million,
Next Stop
Grand
Central,*
and *What
Pete Ate
From
A to Z.*

She lives
in New York City where
she is a founder of the illustrious
Rubber Band Society. She has two
children and a dog, in that order.